Rain Rain Rivers

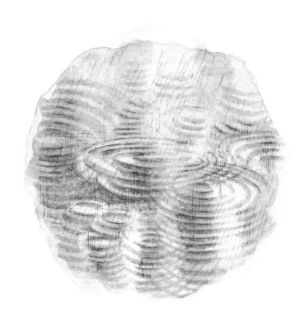

To Dr. Isabel Wright

FROM THE COLLECTION

OF

PETER AND

HELEN

NEUMEYER

Rain Rain Rivers

Words and Pictures by Uri Shulevitz

A Sunburst Book / Farrar, Straus and Giroux

It is raining outside.
I can hear it.

The rain is pattering on the window.

The rain is pattering on the roof.

It rains all over town.

Rain rolls down the roofs,
rushing down the eaves,
gushing out the drainpipes.

Streams stream in the gutters.

Tomorrow I'll sail my little boats.

It rains!
It rains over fields.

It rains over hills.

It rains over grass.

It rains over ponds too.

Frogs,
stop your singing!
Take cover in the water
and listen to the rain.

It pours.

Streams are streaming.

Rills roll down hills,
fall into brooks,
rush into rivers and race to the seas.

Waves billow and roll,
Rush, splash and surge,
Rage, roar and rise.